COLORING BOOK #1

by P.C. Cast

and illustrated by
Aura Dalian

Zoey Redbird – U-we-tsi-a-ge-ya to her grandmother, leader of the Nerd Herd, and beloved daughter to the Goddess, Nyx.

Neferet – ex-High Priestess of Nyx. By embracing Darkness and feeding from the energy of Death, she became immortal Tsi Sgili, and self-proclaimed Goddess of Darkness.

Stevie Rae – the first Red Vampyre High Priestess, and Zoey's BFF.
Gifted with an earth affinity by Nyx.

Aphrodite LaFont – Prophetess of Nyx whose visions, along with her unique form of wisdom, help Zoey restore the balance of Light and Darkness.

Damien – gifted with an affinity for air by Nyx, he loves playing the role of teacher to the Nerd Herd.

The Twins – whether they are together or separate, their elements,
fire and water, bind them to the Nerd Herd.

The Nerd Herd!

Nyx, Goddess of Night, Patroness of Vampyres and all who choose Light over Darkness.

Kalona – brother to Erebus, fallen Warrior and Guardian of Nyx.

Mother Earth – her creative power is symbolized in the form of a powerful
and beautiful pregnant woman, flanked the sun and moon.

House of Night familiars. Can you name them all?

Big Bonnie – Travis's beautiful and faithful Percheron mare.

Dragon Lankford's Maine Coon, Shadowfax, with his forever mate, Anastasia's sweet Guinevere.

A ritual table made ready for a Full Moon Ritual, laden with spirit candle, athame, wine-filled chalice, an image of the Goddess, and the bounty of the latest harvest. Blessed be!

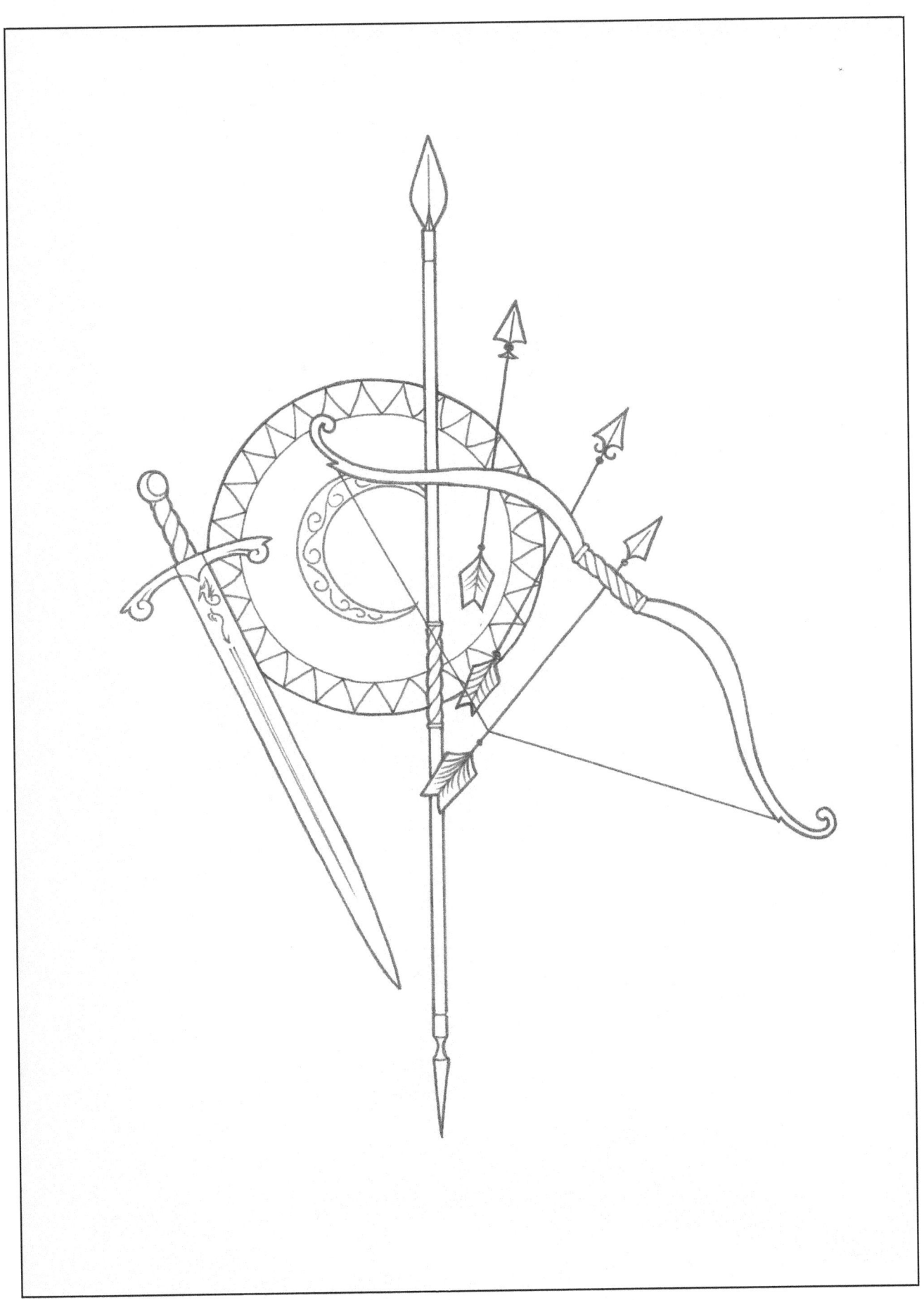

Traditional House of Night weaponry: Stark's bow, Kalona's spear, and Dragon Lankford's sword and shield.

Grandma Redbird's dream catcher, woven with love and positive energy, bejeweled with turquoise, and decorated with dove's feathers and lavender.

The pentagram is an ancient symbol of the position of the five elements: air, fire, water, earth, and spirit.

The goddess within the bull is ancient symbolism for the balance of Light and Darkness.

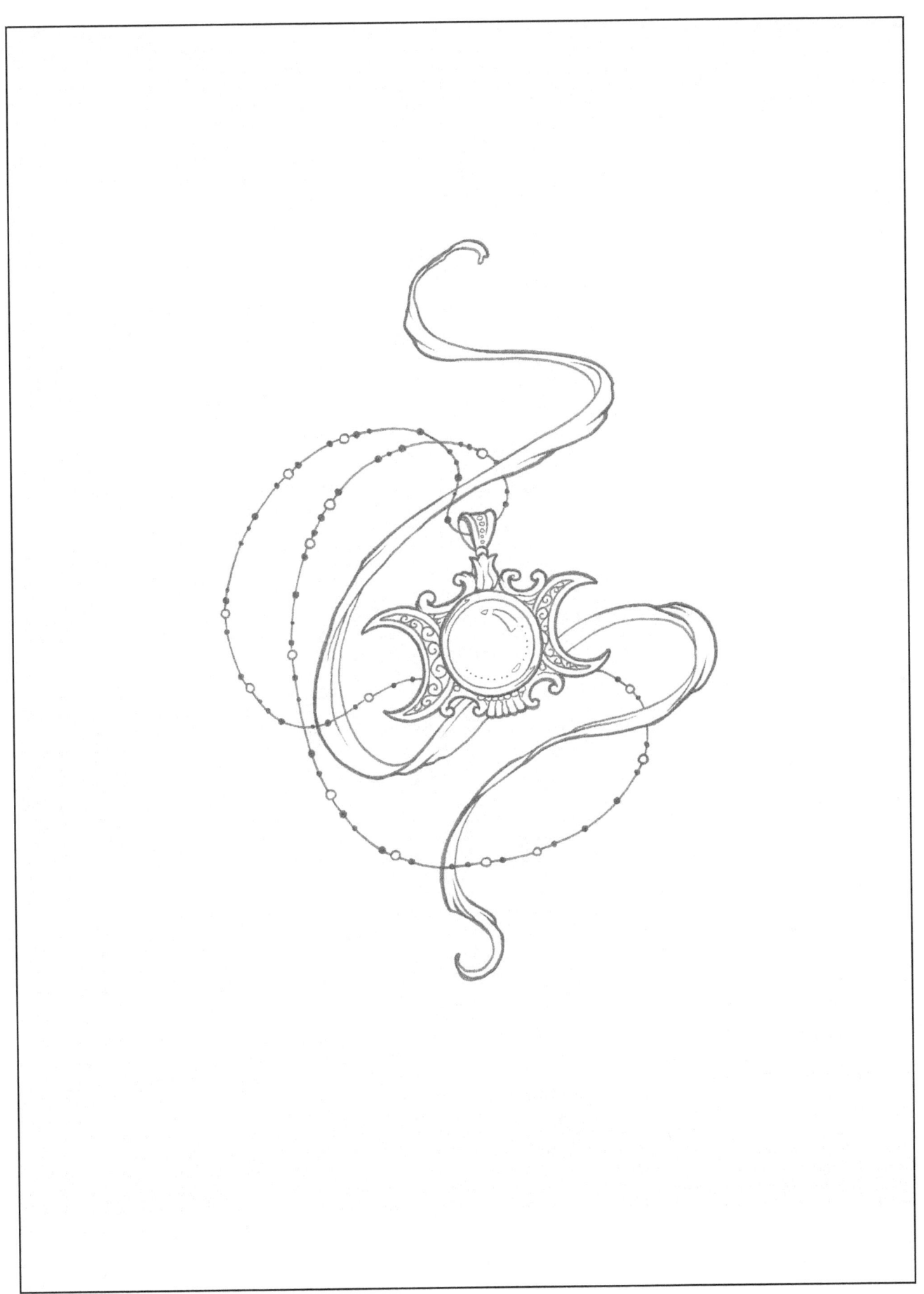

The triple moon pendant worn by the Leader of the Dark Daughters.

A House of Night Yule tree, decorated by fledglings with candles and gifts
of popcorn and cranberries for Tulsa's squirrels and birds.

A House of Night statue of Nyx, Goddess of Night.

The wishing tree from the entrance of Nyx's Otherworld.

Zoey's 1966 VW Bug with a dream catcher made by Grandma Redbird decorating the rearview mirror.

A scene from Betrayed when Zoey rides Persephone through the snowstorm to rescue Heath in the tunnels under the depot.

Zoey in the Goddess Glen in the Otherworld after Heath's death shattered her soul.

Empowered once more, Zoey leading a Full Moon Ritual.

The tunnels under the depot, filled with the feral red fledglings who had lost their humanity.

Neferet in her Tsi Sgili form of a spider, spinning evil in her web of Darkness.

Rephaim the Raven Mocker, before he found his humanity through Stevie Rae's love.

Castle of Sgiach, the Great Taker of Heads, on the Scottish Isle of Skye.

Tulsa's House of Night.

Tattoos

Lenobia's Mark

Dragon Lankford's Mark

James Stark's Mark

HOUSE OF NIGHT CROSSWORD

ACROSS

7 KNOWN AS THE HIGH PRIESTESS OF DEATH
8 STONE OF PROTECTION
13 LEADER OF THE BENEDICTINE NUNS
14 ELEMENT OF THE SOUTH
15 KEY HERB IN A CLEANSING SMUDGE STICK
16 ZOEY'S FAVORITE CEREAL
18 ZOEY'S FAVORITE DRINK
19 FAVORITE APHRODITE SAYING
22 SHE MEOWS LIKE A GRUMPY OLD WOMAN
23 THE STRENGTH OF A PROTECTIVE SPELL DEPENDS
   UPON THE _____ OF THE HIGH PRIESTESS CASTING
   THE SPELL
24 SYMBOLIZES THE ANCIENT FORCES OF DARKNESS
26 ELEMENT OF THE WEST
27 IS RESPONSIBLE FOR MARKING FLEDGLINGS
29 ZOEY'S CAR
30 BELONGS TO APHRODITE
32 GRANDMA'S NICKNAME FOR ZOEY'S WARRIOR
34 HENRIETTA HIGH SCHOOL IS HOME OF THE
   FIGHTING ____

DOWN

1 ELEMENT OF THE CIRCLE'S CENTER
2 KALONA'S FAVORITE SON
3 THE STEP-LOSER
4 CHEROKEE WORD FOR DAUGHTER
5 LOCATION OF NEFERET'S PENTHOUSE
6 ELEMENT OF THE EAST
9 THE MAGICKAL BOND THAT SOMETIMES HAPPENS
   BETWEEN A HUMAN AND A VAMPYRE
10 ZOEY'S FAVORITE HORSE
11 ZOEY'S FAVORITE BOOK
12 SYMBOLIZES THE ANCIENT FORCES OF LIGHT
13 HOME OF THE VAMPYRE HIGH COUNCIL
17 ZOEY WOULD SAY GEOMETRY IS A BUNCH OF
   BULL_____
20 APHRODITE'S WARRIOR
21 ELEMENT OF THE NORTH
25 ANCIENT HOME OF VAMPYRE HIGH COUNCIL, NOW
   ABANDONED
28 RED FLEDGLING POET LAUREATE
31 RED FLEDGLING GIFTED WITH TRUE SIGHT
33 THE GREAT TAKER OF HEADS

Fan Q&A with PC Cast

I posted on my Facebook and blog asking for fans to submit questions to me, the Q&A to be included in this coloring book. Wow! You guys flooded me! Here are your questions and my answers. Thank you for such a smart, interesting dialogue. HoN fans are awesomesauce!

XXXOOO
PC

Q: Alltimemusic asked: "What got you into writing? Tips for newbies?"

A: I can't remember not reading or writing. Some of my very earliest memories are of my parents reading me *Johnny Go Round* by Betty Ren Wright. It was published four months before I was born, so I'm guessing that memory is pretty old! My family and extended family are big readers. Books have been part of my life since my childhood. I grew up reading about great adventures, and making up equally great adventures in my mind. I thought everyone did that! I also thought everyone wrote those stories down. I wrote my first story down in first grade – *Blubby the Blue Whale* (no, it's not published!). And I kept writing my stories down, and rewriting them, and writing more stories, and then rewriting them. I'm still doing it!

My biggest piece of advice for aspiring authors is to treat the job of being a writer as you would any other career. Research the business of publishing. Hone your writing skills. Seek out creative writing classes and writers' groups. Read everything you can get your hands on. Then write. And rewrite. Then write some more. There is no magic pill you can take that will suddenly make you an author. First, you have to attain the skills you need to tell a story, and then you need to be tenacious. On my blog I dedicate an entire post in the archives wherein I list books geared to help aspiring authors. Good luck!

p.s. Go to book signings! Not to ask the author for anything – just go and buy a book from a real person while you envision signing your own books. (I think it builds up good karma for authors to attend book signings.)

Q: Johan B asked: "Where did you draw inspiration for the Bull legends?"

A: I drew inspiration from the ancient Irish myth that tells the story of two powerful Druids, eternally in conflict. As the eons passed, they shifted form, finally becoming enormous, powerful bulls whose horns were locked together in a never-ending battle.

Q: Brittany C asked: "I'm sure that many of us while reading the books have screamed out "why is she doing this to the characters!" Have you ever found your own self doing the same while writing?

A: All the time! My characters often do things that surprise and upset me. There are usually at least one or two points in each book when I'm bawling while I'm writing. When Jack died? SNOT CRY.

Q: Felicia G asked: "If you were Marked as a fledgling, what are some of the classes at the House of Night that you'd like to be enrolled in? Also, if Marked, what goddess given affinity would you like to have?

A: Oooh! Good questions! I would definitely enroll in the equestrian class. I'm a big rider, and I heart me some Lenobia! I'd also take drama, spells and rituals, and definitely Spanish because my Spanish sucks. Like Zoey, I'd avoid anything that has to do with math.

As for my element – it would have to be earth.

Q: Michelle M asked: "What inspired you to write about teenage vampyres? I love the story lines and how you made the characters in "todays" world..."

A: In 2005 my fabulous agent and friend, Meredith Bernstein, and I were having dinner at a Romance Writers of America National Convention and she said that she had an idea for a series she would like to see me write. I asked about her idea, and she said three words that changed my life: vampire finishing school. I had been teaching high school English for about ten years then, so I immediately thought of a YA setting. Meredith wasn't so sure, as YA hadn't become a hot selling genre yet, but she believed in me, and she knew that I understood teenagers. She told me to write the first three chapters of the series and we'd see what would happen. St. Martin's Press saw something special in those three chapters, and you guys know the rest of the story!

Q: Shayla B asked: "How did you come up with the magical House of Night world?!"

A: After my agent asked me to write a series set at a vampire finishing school, I decided to make MY vampyres (with a y!) different than any others. My first step was to make their society matriarchal, because that is where my writing has always trended. Then I looked to biology as the basis for my vamps, which means I called my dad. Dad taught biology for about a zillion years, and he has long been my go-to guy for anything to do with ecology, botany, geology, biology or physiology in my worlds (Partholon fans can thank Dad for the fact that that world has a functioning ecosystem, and that centaurs are physiologically sound – if you add fantasy to physiology). So I told Dad what I wanted – unique vampyre physiology, and I also knew it had to be linked to hormones (I was writing about teenagers!) and I thought it would be smart to use DNA and pheromones. Dad came up with the biology that made it work. Thanks, Mighty Mouse! I love you!

Q: Charlotte P asked: "When you created the characters did you have an inspiration in mind, someone to base the characters off of?"

A: I was teaching high school at South Intermediate High in Broken Arrow as I was writing the first four House of Night books, so many of the characters, and the issues they deal with, were inspired by teaching for more than a decade. Sometimes I used a student's name. Sometimes I used a physical description of a student. But what always happened is once I began writing, that "student" became a House of Night character, and took on his or her own, fictional, personality. A prime example of this is Zoey herself. I based Zoey on Kristin when she was about sixteen years old. But the Z you guys know in the series is a totally different character than Kristin. Yes, she looks like Kristin, and she has some of her idiosyncrasies (Kristin loves Count Chocula, brown pop, and is a non-curser), but the HoN Zoey and Kristin have little else in common, as they have both matured and grown into unique individuals.

Q: Rebekah M.S. asked: "I love how you mix different cultures and religion in the book. How were you inspired to do this? Was there any reason behind it, such as your own religious or cultural background?"

A: My inspiration was rooted in frustration that grew out of the closed-minded, Bible Belt mindset. I just got sick of it. I disliked what judgment and exclusion was doing to the young people around me. I saw how destructive the THERE IS ONLY ONE RIGHT ANSWER AND I HAVE IT belief system was/is to our world. So, I began to write, creating a society wherein teenagers and adults had the opportunity to break free from that mindset and live a different destiny.

Q: Elizabeth H asked: "Dose your daughter help you with your ideas?"

A: Yes and no. I do all the writing, and then I turn the manuscripts in to Kristin. She serves as my teen voice editor. It's easier for her to work if she doesn't know what's going to happen in the novels. It gives her an unbiased, fresh perspective. So I don't brainstorm with her. But I do get her input after I've written the first draft, and I value that input greatly. Kristin is an excellent editor!

Q: Hannah R asked: "Who is your favorite character in the book and why?"

A: That is a hard choice! I can tell you who is the most fun to write – Aphrodite! I identify with her closely. I also identify with Lenobia very closely as well. Neferet's point of view used to be a lot of fun to write, but as her character became darker, her point of view became more and more difficult to write. Grandma Redbird is another one of my favorites. As for the male characters, Damien and Heath make me smile a lot.

Q: Stephanie B asked: "Did you ever image you'd influence your daughter so much? And do you think you'll start another series?"

A: Of course I thought I'd influence my daughter so much – I'm her mother! Well, okay, I didn't actually think she'd be a novelist, though. I was hoping she'd be a veterinarian. Kristin Cast, DMV, still sounds magical to me. Sigh. Anyway, right now she just finished her first solo novel, and it is awesome! So I do think it's cool that she's choosing to be an author, though I honestly didn't expect it.

Will I start another series? Absolutely! I'm already outlining it and asking Dad for biology help!

Q: Abby R asked: "Where is your favorite place to write?"

A: I have developed the ability to write anywhere, but I prefer to write in a quiet room, with my crystals and candles and research books. I like to be surrounded by my dogs (who think they're helping me). And I always write on a TreadDesk (google it).

Q: Elayne T asked: "Are many places in the House of Night based on real life Tulsa, Oklahoma?"

A: Oh, heck yes! Zoey's school is the school I taught at for fifteen years, South Intermediate High School (waving to my ex-students!). The setting of the House of Night is based on Cascia Hall, a private school in Midtown, Tulsa. The depot is real, and so are the tunnels under Tulsa, though they don't stretch under the depot and the depot is now the Oklahoma Jazz Hall of Fame. Philbrook Museum and its lovely grounds, including the gazebo, are real. Gilcrease Museum and the Gilcrease house are real. The site of the Benedictine nuns is real, as is Mary's Grotto, and Woodward Park. All the locations at Utica Square are real (and I go there often). I do heart me some Andolini's Pizza! I've walked the ruins of Sgiach's Castle on the Isle of Skye in Scotland. I've visited San Clemente Island, off the coast of Venice. Actually, there are more "real" places in the HoN than fictional ones!

Q: Selene P. D. asked, "When you write do you always secretly hide yourself in your characters?"

A: Selene, that question made me laugh out loud! I don't think I do anything "secretly" in my writing! My friends, family, and even acquaintances all know that I cannibalize my life for my books. There are pieces of my past, present, future, dreams, fears, desires, nightmares, *everything* in my books. Nothing is taboo. It's embarrassing but true that in my first published novel, DIVINE BY MISTAKE, the heroine is blatantly me. Basically, I took myself on a magnificent adventure. My writing has matured since then, but I am willing to use anything and everything in my life to get my stories told. It's one reason I never read reviews.

Q: Sarah G.T. asked, "Will you write more books related to the House of Night world, like prequels or anything like that?"

A: Right now I don't have any planned. Actually right now I'm outlining and world building a new series. But you never know. I may revisit the HoN if I believe there is a story left untold.

Q: Christine C asked, "When you're having a bad day, does it help to get lost in your writing?"

A: Actually, yes, it does. Writing quiets the babble in my head. It's also an escape. When I'm really into a manuscript it feels just like it does when I'm reading an awesome book, and I definitely escape into my own world.

Q: Bobbie H. O. asked: "If you could talk to any writer living or dead who would it be and why?"

A: Bobbie, may I choose two writers? If so, I would invite Ray Bradbury and Anne McCaffrey to share a multi-course dinner with me, complete with lots and lots of excellent wine. Then I would just sit back and observe those two brilliant and unique authors as they laughed and talked. I would be honored to host them.

I used to say that I believed every American should read *Fahrenheit 451*. As I have matured and, hopefully, gained wisdom, I have changed my belief. Now I believe everyone who loves freedom of thought and speech needs to read *Fahrenheit 451*. The country you call home is far less important than your core values, and your inalienable right to express them. That is something we can all share with Mr. Bradbury.

It is because of Anne McCaffrey's Pern that I realized a woman could write *and* star in a science fiction/fantasy novel. Ms. McCaffrey gave me the courage to take the leap from daydreamer to novelist. I didn't get the opportunity to meet her in person, but she did read my early work. She was gracious and kind and wise, and I owe her a debt of gratitude for her advice. Anne McCaffrey personified the matriarchal, creative soul that lives within an otherwise patriarch-defined genre.

Can you imagine the dinner? I can! Bradbury and McCaffrey bring the stories and the brilliance. I get to bring the wine and reap the benefits!

Q: Steph A. asked, "Is there ever going to be a movie out about HoN? If there is, will it follow the books as closely as possible, and will it be one book at a time or two together?"

A: The HoN has been optioned by Davis Films. The reason I choose them was because I liked the vision they had of a HoN movie franchise, making multiple movies that are unique, and yet still maintain the soul of my world. I am not a screenwriter, nor am I a producer, so I cannot promise that Samuel Hadida will keep his word to me, but I do honestly believe he shares my vision. The movies will be different than the books. It simply does not make sense any other way. First person novels do not translate literally to film, and the first several books are first person from Zoey's point of view. What makes sense to me is to combine several of the early books into the first movie, and interpret the later books more literally. I'm looking forward to it!

Q: Brandy U asked, "How old were you when you decided to write the House of Night novels for your fans?"

A: I started writing the HoN in 2005 when I was 45 years young!

Q: Stacey M. asked, "When you write the characters in the books, how far back do you go with their back stories in your mind? Would you ever consider making novellas or short stories about each character of Zoey's circle?"

A: When I create a character I create an entire backstory for him/her. I know all sorts of things about the character that never appear in any book; it helps the character come alive for me. It's also how the HoN novellas came into being. I was having dinner with my publishing family at St. Martin's Press, and someone said something about Anastasia and Dragon Lankford (my publishing team are big HoN fans). I made a comment about Anastasia being older than Dragon, and that they met when he was a fledgling and she was a young professor. I remember there was a big, shocked silence at the table, and then my late, much-missed publisher, Matthew Shear, asked, "Do you know the backstories for all of these characters?" I said, "Yep!" He said, "Can you write them?" I remember that I laughed and said, "Well, I could if my publisher could ease up on my deadlines and give me time to write them." Matthew said, "Done!" And then I outlined and wrote the four HoN novellas, DRAGON'S OATH, LENOBIA'S VOW, NEFERET'S CURSE, and KALONA'S FALL.

Would I consider writing novellas or short stories about Zoey's circle? Probably not novellas, but I might consider some short stories. Stark's past would be especially interesting to fill you guys in on!

Q: Summer O'R asked, "Did you have an obsession for vampires before writing this?"

A: Nope. I had read some vampire novels, but I was/am far from being obsessed. I especially like Anne Rice, and remember reading INTERVIEW WITH A VAMPIRE the year it came out. It scared the bejezzas out of me. I'm also a fan of the vampires created by Chelsea Quinn Yarbro, Annette Curtis Klause, and the fabulous Robin McKinley.

The truth is, I don't spend a lot of time thinking about vampyres. I think of the HoN as being filled with complex, living, breathing characters. Then I think about the matriarchal society I created for them, and the rules of my universe. The fact that they're vampyres is only one part of that complex universe.

Q: Mike G asked, "Which of the many romances in the series is your favorite?"

A: Stevie Rae and Rephaim! I have a soft spot for *Beauty and the Beast* themes.

Q: Alison P asked, "How long is a familiar cat's lifespan? This always bugged me! Are the able to live as long as their vamp? (I know Neferet's first didn't.) Does a vamp have multiple familiars at different points in their lives? How has the series changed from your original ideas once you started writing?"

A: Vampyre familiars do live longer than a normal cat's lifespan, but, sadly, they aren't as long lived as vampyres. Yes, a vampyre will often get chosen by several cats during his or her long life, but usually only one at a time – though that rule has been known to be broken, especially if one cat becomes ill. Another will sometimes choose the vampyre so that the beloved cat's death is easier to bear, though it is always heartbreaking.

The series has changed a lot from the original first three books. When the third book, CHOSEN, debuted #2 on the *New York Times* bestseller list, my publisher opened up my creative floodgates. He contracted me for nine more books, and then he said I could expand the world and write *anything I wanted to write!* And I certainly did. I got to delve into the mythos of the world and set up an epic struggle against Light and Darkness. I also got to follow secondary storylines, which is how I was able to introduce Kalona, Rephaim, Thanatos, Kramisha, Shaylin, Dallas, Nicole, Sgiach...and many others!

Q: Katie L asked, "How did you get started as an author? How long does it normally take for you to complete a book?"

A: As I said earlier, I've been writing for as long as I remember, but I got serious about finishing a novel-length piece of work in my late thirties. So, I decided to write the book I most wanted to read - a fun, sexy fantasy set in an alternative universe where the heroine (basically, me) was mistaken for a goddess. I made several very, very bad attempts at writing the manuscript before I found my voice and my plot. Then, even though I was teaching English and didn't need an undergrad class, I enrolled in a creative writing class at OSU-Tulsa, taught by the fabulously talented, and very patient, Teresa Miller. Using those weekly classes as my pretend deadlines, and Teresa as my pretend editor, I finished the manuscript. I sold it to a small, regional press. It totally shocked me by getting great reviews and winning several national romance and science fiction/fantasy awards. I was able to gain the attention of one of the top literary agents in New York, Meredith Bernstein. Within a week of signing with Meredith, I had a three book contract with Berkley Publishing. It was my eighteenth published novel that hit the *New York Times* bestseller list. I taught at South Intermediate High School for fifteen years while I wrote full time for Berkley, Harlequin, and St. Martin's Press. No, I didn't sleep much.

It takes me anywhere from one year to four months to write a book. It depends on the book. Some go faster than others. I like having a year to write a book. I rarely manage to convince publishers to give me that year...

Q: Erin M asked, "What gave you the idea for the Red Vampires?"

A: As I expanded the HoN world I began to delve more fully into the idea that there should always be a balance of Light and Darkness, good and evil. That led me to explore the nature of humanity, and how that balance, or unbalance, could affect my characters. I was especially intrigued by whether, once lost, humanity could be regained. All of that thinking and wondering led me to create the red vampyres – or more accurately – they created themselves during my thinking and wondering.

Q: Ariel B asked, "Are you going to create another supernatural romance series?"

A: I'm definitely going to create another series, and my favorite genre to write is fantasy mixed with science fiction. Because I think life is more intriguing when you add romance to it, I can promise you there will be plenty of romance in the series!

Q: Amberly H asked, "If you could go back and change the story, would you, and what changes would you make?"

A: Amberly, I am a chronic rewriter. If I could go back and change ANY of my books, I would. I would continually tinker with them, writing and rewriting, changing, expanding, deleting, etc., AND NOTHING WOULD EVER GET PUBLISHED. Seriously. I avoid rereading my books once they're in print, because I always find things I wish I could change. When I need to reread books in a series, I do so by listening to the audio versions. That's easier for me to bear.

Q: Christina S asked, "Why do you wanna end HON? Can't you keep writing them?"

A: Well, I suppose I could keep writing the HoN books, but I've told the story in my head, so it's time to move on to new worlds and characters and stories.

Q: Marisa S asked, "First off, I'm so excited for this! I have always loved the art of the books and I'm looking forward to getting this little book of beautiful in my hands! Your characters are so developed, each possesses a very unique personality. Do the characters just appear in your mind and share their nuances, or do they make you ferret out each trait that makes them who they are? I can't wait! Brightest blessings upon you and yours."

A: Thank you Marisa! Characters evolve in different ways. Sometimes I get the character before the story begins. That's how I got Zoey. I knew her before I knew the plot of the HoN. I based her on Kristin, and then she took on a life of her own. Sometimes I have a plot idea, and need to develop a character for the plot, which is what happened with Kalona. I knew I wanted to introduce a fallen immortal who had to struggle with redemption. So, I began researching ancient myths and legends – everything from the Lucifer story to tales of the Greek gods. Out of my research, Kalona took form. And sometimes characters just appear as I'm writing – like Stark. He showed up and I thought he was going to fall for Stevie Rae. Well, Stark had other plans!

Q: Breanna N.S. asked, "What has been your favorite part of writing and creating House of Night?"

A: I have loved the maturation of the characters. I hadn't written about such young characters before, and it has been very satisfying to watch them grow up and learn and change.

Q: Maya R asked, "Why do the vampires have tattoos? How did you come up with that? (It's super awesome:))"

A: I gave my vampyres tattooed Marks as a loving and respectful nod to ancient priestesses who marked their bodies when they dedicated their lives to follow the path of their goddess.

Q: Shivani K asked, "Do you have weird motivations or like little rituals when you come up with new ideas or before you start writing?"

A: Hum...well, I guess maybe I do. I clear my writing space/office between each manuscript. I light candles (usually vanilla scented). I arrange some cool crystals on my desk, and other knickknacks I find inspirational. I make sure I have a lot of research books on tables nearby. I usually drink herbal or green tea – lots of it. I write at night. And I always write on a TreadDesk.

Q: Shelby M asked, "What book was the hardest book to write? Has writing with your daughter strengthened your relationship with her?"

A: NEFERET'S CURSE was the most difficult book to write. When I was a teenager I was date raped. It wasn't as brutal as what happened to Neferet, and it wasn't by a family member, but I did draw from my experience to get into Neferet's head so that my readers could understand why Neferet made the choices she did. I'm pleased with the book, but writing it was not a pleasant experience.

I don't actually write with Kristin. I do all the writing, and Kristin serves as my teen voice editor. Kristin and I have always had a very close relationship, so that hasn't changed. What has changed, though, is my respect for her professionally. Kristin is an excellent editor! Her gut instincts are right. When she tells me something needs to be cut, I listen to her (even though I don't want to). And it's much more fun to tour with Kristin than to tour by myself!

Q: Amanda L asked, "I have a question for you P.C. Of all of the gods and goddesses from all different places, how and why did you use Nyx? What is it about Nyx in particular drew you to her?"

A: That's easy! I read this quote by Hesiod, and I knew Nyx was the right goddess for my series, and that I had my title!

"There also stands the gloomy house of Night;
ghastly clouds shroud it in darkness.
Before it Atlas stands erect and on his head
and unwearying arms firmly supports the broad sky,
where Night and Day cross a bronze threshold
and then come close and greet each other."

Q: Kamille K asked, "What's it like getting attached to some characters, and then having to kill them off, or finally having the series end?"

A: I make myself bawl when cool characters die! I don't see it as me killing them off. It's part of the plot and I'm just recording what the characters are doing inside my head. I didn't want Dragon or Jack or Heath or Erin or...well, lots of other characters, to die either!

It's weird having the series end. I've been living with these characters for almost a decade. They've been a very real part of my life. I'm going to miss them, but I'm satisfied that I have told their story to the best of my abilities.

Q: Tiffaney G asked, "I adore your books...all the different series, and have even gotten my husband pretty hooked as well. I have tons of questions, but here are some that others didn't already ask.

I know it's hard to imagine these characters any other way, but if things were different, simpler even, so you think they'd have been drawn together the same way? Or would Zoey be riding horses and living a more normal, quiet life? Did you even envision other destinies for your characters?

Do you have any tattoos?

If you could step into the life of one of your characters who and when?

If/when the movie is made will you two make an appearance? Pretty please?"

A: Tiffaney, you make me smile. If Zoey hadn't been Marked I imagine she would have become a veterinarian and married Heath. They would have had three little girls, and they would have lived happily ever after.

Yes, I have a lot of body art. Aura Dalian, the illustrator of this beautiful coloring book, is my tattoo artist. I have a giant (and very colorful) dragon that stretches from my left arm all the way down my back. On my other side I have two bulls flanking a goddess. I also have a tattoo, much like the goddess within the bull Aura created for this book, on my left thigh. And I'm considering more body art. Oh, and I didn't get my first tattoo until four years after I began writing the House of Night.

If I could step into one of my character's lives (from the HoN) it would be Lenobia as she was discovering that Travis was Martin finally finding her again.

OF COURSE KRISTIN AND I WILL HAVE CAMEOS IN THE MOVIES! We're looking forward to it!

Q: Jessica B asked, "Why did you choose the Cherokee Tribe for the Novels?"

A: Kristin is of Cherokee descent, and the Trail of Tears ends in Tahlequah, Oklahoma, so it felt like a natural fit for Zoey.

Q: Ashley M asked, "I remember you saying a few times that you don't have writers block, and although many times writing can be hard, and the words don't always flow as freely, you push through because, Duh, it's your job and you have bills (As a 24 yr old, I can no longer deny that this bill thing really exists). So when starting a new story/series, how do you know the difference between pushing through the "writers block" of a great story because you have to, and writing isn't all roses and peonies, and a story that may not be meant for you to write "right now", or even at all?"

A: That's an excellent question! I outline before I write, so that gets me past the initial stage of figuring out whether an idea can be turned into a manuscript. If I can't get the outline written, then it's usually a crappy idea. So I start over with a new, hopefully less crappy idea. After the outline is finished I begin writing by following it, but as I write the characters take over and often do things I never expect them to (I did NOT plan for Stevie Rae or Jack to die). After writing 30+ books I've learned that if, no matter how many times I rewrite a scene, it's just not working, then it is time for me to go back to my outline and make some major changes because that part of the plot wasn't meant to be. It sucks when that happens. Big time.

Q: Kyla S asks, "What do you want readers to learn from your books?"

A: From the HoN I'd like readers to learn acceptance and tolerance for different cultures and religions. I'd like them to realize we are not defined by our sexual preferences, the color of our skin, or the god/goddess to whom we do/don't pray. We are defined by the choices we make. And I would like my HoN readers to believe that the strongest force in the universe is love, always love.

Q: Ardra P asked, "Will you continue writing?"

A: Always. I promise.

HOUSE OF NIGHT CROSSWORD

1 SPIRIT
2 REPHAIM
3 JOHNHEFFER
4 UWESIAGEYA
5 MAY
6 AIR
7 THANATOS
8 TURQUOISE
9 IMPRINT
10 PERSEPHONE
11 DRACULA
12 BLACKBULL
13 SANCLEMENTEISLAND
14 FIRE
15 SAGE
16 COUNTCHOCULA
17 POOPIE
18 BROWNPOP
19 NORMALISOVERRATED
20 DARIUS
21 EARTH
22 NALA
23 INTENT
24 WHITEBULL
25 CAPRI
26 WATER
27 TRACKER
28 KRAMISHA
29 BUG
30 MALEFICENT
31 SHAYLIN
32 TSITAGAASHAYA
33 SGIACH
34 HENS

Author Bio:

P.C. Cast is the #1 New York Times and #1 USA Today best selling author of the phenomena that is the HOUSE OF NIGHT. She lives in Tulsa with her Scotties, her Warrior, Odin, and a bunch of horses. Currently, she's waiting for another cat to choose her.

Illustrator Bio:

Aura Dalian is from Lithuania and she started her tattoo artists career in Ireland. Now she lives and works in Michigan with her small, lovely family.

www.ingramcontent.com/pod-product-compliance
Lightning Source LLC
Chambersburg PA
CBHW080904120626
46555CB00008B/2944